CW00735216

# BOYS LiKE PiNK

## (AND BLUE TOO!)

BY

ELEANOR JONES

FOR MATILDA, FOR ALWAYS
BEING WHO YOU WANT TO BE.

Boys like BLUE.

Girls like PINK.

Isn't that what everybody thinks?

But boys like you,
can like 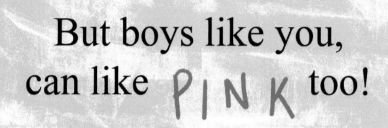 too!

Boys like you can like RED
Just like this hat on a pirate's head.

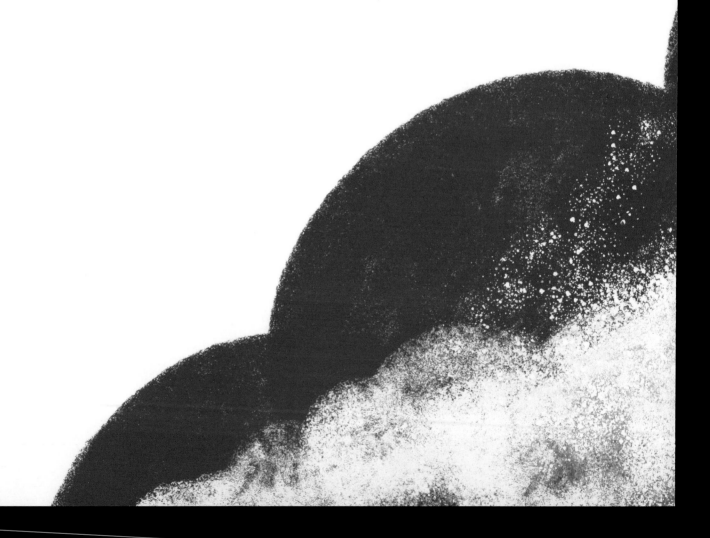

Boys like you can like BLACK
just like the stripes on a zebra's back.

Boys like you can like GREEN
just like the dress on this evil queen.

Boys like you can like 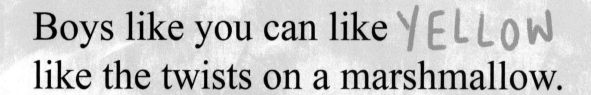 YELLOW
like the twists on a marshmallow.

Boys like you can like WHITE
just like the stars in the night.

Boys can like all the colours,
PINK as much as all the OTHERS!

# ABOUT THE AUTHOR/ILLUSTRATOR

# Eleanor Jones

ELEANOR IS A FREELANCE AUTHOR/ILLUSTRATOR BASED IN SUFFOLK, UK.
FROM A YOUNG AGE ELEANOR SPENT EVERY SPARE SECOND SAT WITH HER PENCILS BUSILY
CREATING CHARACTERS AND SCENES FOR THEM TO EXPLORE!

THIS LOVE OF CREATING CONTINUES TODAY - ELEANOR IS PASSIONATE
ABOUT CREATING CHARACTERS THAT EMPOWER CHILDREN TO BE THEMSELVES AND
SPECIFICALLY TO ALLEVIATE SOME OF THE STEREOTYPING THAT CHILDREN OFTEN FACE,
USING A RANGE OF DIVERSE CHARACTERS TO CHALLENGE THIS.

SINCE QUALIFYING IN EARLY CHILDHOOD EDUCATION ALONGSIDE HER ART STUDIES,
ELEANOR DRAWS FROM HER REAL FIRST HAND EXPERIENCES RELATING TO THE WAY CHILDREN
INTERACT AND PLAY. AS A MOTHER AND AN EDUCATOR, ELEANOR HAS LEARNT A LOT ABOUT
THE THINGS THAT ARE IMPORTANT TO CHILDREN, AS WELL AS THEIR
LEARNING NEEDS - THIS HEAVILY INFLUENCES ELEANOR'S WORK.

Printed in Great Britain
by Amazon